UNWRAPPING HER CURVES

A BBW & QUARTERBACK CHRISTMAS ROMANCE

LANA LOVE

LOVE HEART BOOKS

Also by Lana Love

For a full listing of my books, please visit:

https://www.loveheartbooks.com

v2w

❀ Created with Vellum

CHAPTER 1

MANDY

I'll be lucky to get home by New Year's Eve.

"Hey, Jimmy."

"Where you at, Sis? Should I crack open a beer for you?"

I crane my neck out into the cool afternoon air, then groan.

"I wish. No. I'm still on the freeway. It's…"

"What have I told you about phones while driving? You know how many people I take to the ER because of distracted driving!"

"Whoa. We're at a literal standstill. In fact, my motor is off – just like everyone else. I can't see where the backup even begins. I'm just calling to say I'm going to be phenomenally late."

"Jeez. Sorry. It's just—"

"It's okay. I remember the stories you've told me."

"You should save your phone battery. Text me when it starts clearing and when you have an idea of when you'll arrive. And call me if you need anything." The tone of Jimmy's voice is more somber. It's not the time of year to get stranded on the side of the road. It's not snowy, yet, but it's not at all warm.

"Yes, Dad," I say, a smile spreading across my face. "I'll keep you posted. And don't go bogarting all the beer, 'k?"

SITTING in traffic leaves me alone to think, which is something I've been avoiding lately. The holidays are always hard, primarily because Jimmy and I lost our parents four years ago, thanks to a drunk driver on Christmas Eve. I'm also not as excited as I feel I should be, because my 'I think this guy is the one' boyfriend dumped me three weeks ago.

I know everyone will look at me, that tinge of pity in their eyes when I say that I'm single, *again*. The common refrain will be something like " "You'll find someone when you least expect it!" or "You're smart and pretty...it will work out next time!"

It seems like there's always *next time* on the horizon, when what I really want is to settle down and start a family. No one seems to understand why all of my relationships don't work out — least of all *me*. What's sad, is that I've figured out what the common denominator in all these relationships is – it's me. I don't know how to figure out what's wrong with me, so I can fix it and move on.

Frustration runs through my body and I sit, tense, as I watch the endless lines of red brake lights in front of me. *This traffic jam is not unlike my love life – stalled and going nowhere fast.* I say a little prayer for whatever is causing the traffic jam, because it's likely a serious accident.

I BREATHE an enormous sigh of relief when I pull into my brother's driveway. I need a beer or three after that drive. My gas tank is nearly empty, my butt is sore, and my jacket isn't enough against the chilly wind that blasts me as I hoist my suitcase out of my trunk and rush up to my brother's house. I smile as I knock on the brightly lit front door.

I'm looking forward to moving home in February, and then starting a fresh life. I've been stuck in a pattern of men who aren't right for me and I haven't figured out how to find one who *is* good for me. It's just, sometimes, it's easier to get blinded by lust or dating someone you *think* should be right for you.

I knock on the door hard, again, eager to get inside and see my brother.

When the door opens, my body stops shivering as my libido flares bright enough to heat the whole of Oregon. I blink my eyes rapidly, wondering if car fumes got to me and I'm hallucinating.

"What the hell are *you* doing here?"

CHAPTER 2

TREVOR

*W*ell, hello to you, too, Mandy Hunter. Are you enjoying the holiday season?" I grin, delighting in Mandy's reaction when seeing me. I gave specific instructions for Jimmy not to tell anyone I'd be home this year, but I wasn't sure if he'd actually keep his word on that.

Mandy marches past me, cheeks red from the cold and her eyes bright, and a bolt of desire goes straight to my groin.

Holy fuck.

I knew she was coming, but I didn't realize how amazing she looks now. Our paths haven't crossed in years, since I've always been in a stadium, playing a game on Christmas Day.

If I'd realized Mandy was all sexy and soft curves, I'd have made it back home years ago. She's the one I always wanted, the one who always said no and forever teased me. Fuck. I've spent years fantasizing about her.

"Hey man, close the door! That wind is freezing!"

"Yeah, sorry, Jimmy." I close the door behind me, I turn and see Mandy staring at me.

"Hey, Mandy. How are you? It's been a long time." I move closer to her, to give her a hug, but the expression on her face rapidly cycles between surprise, what I hope is lust, and then a wall comes down in her eyes. Obviously, she has a boyfriend waiting for her or coming along in a day or two. I've heard about her, occasionally, from Jimmy, and there's no way someone as smart and gorgeous as she is could be single.

"Yeah, I'm fine. I..." she mumbles, her blue eyes quickly cutting away from mine. It stings when she looks toward the living room and walks away from me. No one ever walks away from me.

"Sis! You made it!"

"Barely," she sighs, shrugging off her coat and throwing it on a side chair. "Hey Grace. I'm so glad to see you! It's been too long since I saw my best friend!" She gives everyone else a big hug and jealousy rises up in me something fierce.

"It's about time you got home, sis." Jimmy hugs her with one arm and passes her a bottle of beer with the other. "Didn't run out of gas?"

"No," she says. Damn... Watching her tilt that bottle back and take a long drink? A rush of blood goes straight to my groin as I envision her lips wrapped around my cock. Mandy was always sexy, in her shy way, but Jimmy made it damn clear she was off limits.

Now? It's time for the rules to change.

"WHAT *ARE* you doing back here, Trevor? I thought you were living your best life as a famous football player."

I look at Mandy, relieved that she's finally talking to me. We weren't on bad terms last we saw each other, but there's been something dark in her eyes every time I've seen her looking at me tonight. It's like she has a grudge against me, though I know that's impossible. I haven't seen her in years.

"I suppose I was." No matter how many times I'm recognized in public or get interviewed on television, I just feel like me, that talented kid from Gresham. I don't feel like a superstar, though playing pro football has definitely had some Hollywood moments. "I hurt my knee again last month and I'm on the DL. Since I can't play on Christmas, I came home."

"Huh." Mandy's eyes are unreadable, but at least she no longer looks like she wants to kill me. Still, there's a definite distance between us.

"What about you? How you doin' in Seattle?"

"Don't ask." She rolls her eyes and takes another long pull of her beer. "In fact, I dislike it so much, I'm moving back here in February. I wanted to come back earlier, but work locked me into a final project. Honestly, I can't wait to come home, even if it means seeing my obnoxious brother all the time."

Mandy smiles at her brother, leaning over to punch him on the arm. Jimmy laughs, punching her back.

"Yay!" Grace's voice is a screech of excitement and she lunges over to Mandy and gives her a big hug. "You didn't tell me you had a finalized move date! I can't wait for you to be back! You won't regret it, girl, seriously. Oh my God! I can't believe I'm finally getting my BFF back!"

Once again, a shadow falls over her eyes. There's a story she's not telling people. I want to ask her, but I know better than to ask her in front of the others. Though, I tell myself, why would she even talk to me? She has absolutely zero reason to confide in me and with the way she's been looking at me, I seriously doubt she has any plans to.

Maybe she's heard about the reputation I had a few years ago. A lot of money and a lot of fame doesn't lend itself to respectable behavior. I fell into the fame trap that so many of us did – lots of parties, booze, women, money to burn, acting like kings because everyone treated us as kings. Looking back, I'm grateful I didn't get in any trouble and end up with a baby from a woman I didn't remember.

These days, I want a nice quiet life, to give back to the community that helped me become the football player I became. I want to be married and have a big family.

As I watch Mandy relax in front of the fireplace, laughing and joking with her brother and Grace, I'm reminded even more why I liked her. She's funny and down to earth, not to mention the shape of her body. I feel damn lucky to be a part of this. She's natural, here, the love for her brother and best friend plain as day remind me why I always found her so compelling.

Mandy is exactly the kind of woman I want for a wife. I finish another beer, then am blindsided by the realization – it's Mandy. It's always been Mandy. Even when she turned me down, time after time in high school, it was always her. Some part of me, deep down, knew that she was the one. She was the only girl I ever longed for enough that I kept asking and asking.

She's the woman I want to be my wife.

CHAPTER 3

MANDY

*O*h, no...I don't think about Trevor...” Grace says, nearly falling on the floor because she's laughing so hard. “Mandy, babe, you should hear yourself. I don't need a polygraph to know you're lying when you say that!”

“Well...maybe,” I finally concede. “Okay, maybe a lot. But you know how it is! He's on TV, he's in the paper, he's in magazines. Like chunky me would ever have a chance with him. As if!”

I drain the rest of my beer and motion to the bartender to bring us two new beers.

“Again, with the lies! Don't think I've forgotten how he chased after you in high school or how you teased him. He wanted you *bad* and I know how hard you crushed on him.”

“You of all people know how much I wanted him back then. But he was so busy having everyone else and was so famous for never dating a girl for more than one or two weeks.”

I look away from Grace and lose myself in the memories from high school. Me, being the 'girl with a pretty face,' but not 'the girl that every guy wants to date.' It's not that I was even that much overweight, but that I wasn't as skinny as the popular girls. And for that, I was never fully part of the in crowd. I wasn't with the outcasts or the loners, but I was in that weird middle ground of 'not quite good enough.'

Aside from my work, most of my life has felt like 'not quite good enough.' I've certainly felt that way with men, who inevitably dump me and said cliché things like "you're really pretty" or "I'm just not ready for a relationship" or "you haven't done anything wrong." And then I run into them six months or maybe a year later and what's the status then? They're engaged. They're recently married. It always leaves me feeling like shit.

"Girl, I think you did the right thing in high school. He was too popular for his own good. Despite how much he obviously wanted you, he would've broken your heart like he did with all the other girls."

"Maybe you're right. But I'm still the same. Since he went pro, all he's had are a string of flings or high-profile girlfriends. And we both know that I can't fill those kinds of shoes. Or rather, I can't fit in those kinds of dresses."

"I don't know, Mandy. You shouldn't be so down on yourself." The look in Grace's eyes changes to the look of concern that she gives me every time the subject of me and men come up. Her telling me how beautiful I am and how amazing I am, in an attempt to boost my self-esteem, is a well-worn talk that I don't believe anymore. It's not like I don't know these things, but it's hard to believe them when I have yet to meet a man who feels the same way.

"I know what you're going to say, Grace, and I love you for it, I really do. But I've just been dumped yet again. So, yeah. My self-esteem has taken yet another beating."

Sadness and anger flip across Grace's eyes as she watches me. "Are you okay? You didn't even tell me that you were dating anyone."

I sigh and silently curse how beer loosened me up enough to admit this. My mind plays the highlights reel of my short relationship with Robert. We had our good moments. He knew how to make me laugh, but he didn't like taking me out with his friends or with his coworkers.

"Things weren't always great between us. I liked Robert, but I think I probably knew that it would never work out with him, but I still hoped. When I asked about his corporate Christmas party, he got all weird and said they couldn't bring dates. I think he just meant he was embarrassed to be seen with me."

"What a bastard!" Grace is suitably outraged on my behalf and as much as I didn't want to tell the story, her having my back and denouncing Robert does make me feel a little better.

"Pretty much."

"Have I mentioned he's a fucking asshole? Oh!" Grace exclaims, her eyes glittering with calculation, "that just means that now is the best time to have a fling. And who better to have a fling with than Trevor Collins? I'd bet my right arm that he would make you feel ah-mazing. I saw how he was looking at you last night. He couldn't take his eyes off you."

"There's way too much history there. He's my brother's best friend and I'll definitely see him in the future. I don't need to add to my future stress. Plus, you know I'm not the type to have flings with men." A hazy lust-dream settles in my mind – Trevor, naked and smiling in my bed, his hand outstretched to me in invitation, me taking his hand, and then me losing myself in him and making every sexual fantasy I've ever had a reality.

"And that there is a damn shame, Mandy Hunter."

"No fair that you get the pro football player on your team!" I yell at my brother, pretending I'm upset.

We're choosing sides for our annual flag football game. The sun is as high in the sky as it gets in December, but it's the prettiest, clearest day I've seen in weeks. Bright blue skies, a not-too-cold breeze, no hint of rain or snow in the air.

"You gave me first pick. What did you think was going to happen?" He puts his hands on his hips and smiles gleefully at me. "Besides, I'm not an idiot. I know how fast you run!"

"Are you saying you want me?" Trevor teases, walking over to me. I jump when his hand slides down my back and dangerously close to my ass.

"What gave you *that* idea?" I faux-pout at him as I dance away from his hand. Trevor's caress triggers a fresh wave of desire in me and I really want to tackle him…naked.

At halftime, Jimmy passes around a couple of thermoses filled with rum-laced hot chocolate. The alcohol warms my body and helps me to relax a little. Every time I get close to Trevor, I fumble and stumble because I'm so distracted by his tall, muscular body. No matter how much I tell myself to stop with all the fantasies, I can't deny that I'm more attracted to him than I was in high school – and that's saying something!

"Alright! For the win!" Jimmy dances around on the field, celebrating that he and Trevor are up by ten points.

"Yeah, yeah. Just you wait," I taunt, putting my hands on my hips. "Grace and I are going to destroy you."

Jimmy looks at Trevor, and then busts out laughing. "Yeah right, little sis. You're playing against two pro football players!"

"Two? I think you're mistaken there, dear brother. Because from where I'm standing, I only see one pro."

"Fine. If it wasn't for this damn shoulder, I would've been. You know that."

"Coulda woulda shoulda." I laugh in the cool breeze, walking over to where Trevor and Jimmy are standing, ready to start the second half of the game.

Jimmy lowers his eyes at me and I know he's going to come at me hard. We start the second half and Grace and I nearly tie up the score.

"Just admit it, Mandy," Trevor says joining in with Jimmy and heckling Grace and me. "You know we're going to win."

We'll see about that. The play starts and Jimmy sprints with the ball. I chase after him as fast as I can, but Trevor steps in front of me suddenly and blocks me. I slam into his body and we both go flying onto the ground, and I land on top of his strong body.

"Oof!" The air goes out of my lungs and it takes me a hot second to realize that I am on top of Trevor Collins. A million thoughts run through my mind, namely that I must be crushing him. "I…um… Sorry about that. I didn't mean to tackle you. But you just got in my way."

I squirm to try and move away from him and stand up, but he grips my arms. I can't move.

"I was just doing my job and blocking you." Then in a quieter voice, he adds, "but if this is what it takes to get close to you, then I'll step in front of you every time I see you. You can tackle me any time. Any time at all."

"I think you should let me get up, so that we can continue the game," I say, flustered. Of all the ways I imagined being body to body with Trevor, this isn't what I imagined.

"But what if I don't want to let you go? I've always wanted you. You know that."

The tone of Trevor's voice has a seriousness I've rarely heard. Even though the warning bells in my mind are telling me to run away, I just want to sink into something with Trevor — preferably a bed.

"I don't know…" There aren't many times in my life where I've been at a loss for words, but I can't think of anything coherent to say. I can hear Grace and Jimmy laughing and talking, but I can't register the actual words. Right now, my whole world is what Trevor is saying to me and the way his body feels under mine.

Trevor and I stand up, but we can't stop looking at each other.

"Are you okay?" Trevor's voice is gentle and it sends a whole new set of emotions in motion for me. He's always been brash and arrogant, but there's a tenderness right now that hits deep inside of me.

I look away as I brush off my clothing. "I think so, yes. How about you? Did I crush you?"

"I've never been better," he says, looking deep into my eyes. "Let's go for a beer after the game. Just you and me."

A million thoughts race through my mind. I know what he's asking and I know that I should say no, but my body and my self-esteem need this. Maybe I need to abandon my fear of flings and just have a fling with him. I ignore the voice that says "what about when you see him in the future" and smile at him.

"Yes."

CHAPTER 4

TREVOR

This game can't end fast enough.

I want to lose myself in Mandy and her luscious body. I want to hear her sigh and moan as we roll around in bed and take care of what I wish we'd taken care of so many years ago. She said no to me so many times back in the day, that it *really* feels like Christmas has come early. Her saying yes to a drink feels better than winning the Super Bowl.

"What's gotten into you man?" Jimmy asks. "You're barely passing me the ball."

I wipe my arm across my forehead. "I'm scoring, right?"

"Sure. But were supposed to be a team, right?" Jimmy's voice is tight.

"Sorry, man. Next one's yours."

I get the ball and run to the side, easily evading Mandy and Grace. Jimmy runs long and is wide open. I throw the ball to him and it sails perfectly through the air. He's going to make a touchdown easily, because Mandy and Grace are trying to block me and completely ignoring him.

"What?" Grace says, her eyes tracking the ball. "Dammit."

I watch as Jimmy reaches to catch the ball. Mandy is sprinting toward him and she might just catch him.

"Get it, man!" I yell.

Jimmy jumps for the ball, but his timing is off. He stretches for the ball and fumbles it, and I wince as he falls and lands on his arm. Hard.

I immediately run over to Jimmy because I know what a bad fall looks like. He's slow to get up off of the ground and his eyes are screwed up in pain. This isn't good. I recognize how hard he's trying hard to mask his pain, but the way he's swearing shows how badly he's losing the battle.

"Dude. You okay?"

"Jimmy! Are you okay?" Mandy asks, breathless.

Jimmy groans and starts to sit up. "I dislocated my fucking shoulder again." He stands up and wrenches his shoulder back into place, bellowing as he does so. Resetting your own shoulder is excruciating.

"Dude, we need to get you to the hospital."

Jimmy tries to resist, but when he tries to make a fist and only manages to faintly grasp at the air, it's glaringly obvious that he needs the ER.

"That's it. Don't try and argue with me. We're going to the hospital." The look in Mandy's eyes is pained when she sees how much her brother is hurting. She's already walking to the car, assuming that we're following her.

"Fuck, man. I think I pinched a nerve." Jimmy's eyes are rolling back in his head and I wince, worried he's about to pass out. We follow her and she sets off for the hospital like a bat out of hell.

"Almost there, buddy." Mandy speeds through the traffic. Every bump in the road on the way to the hospital makes Jimmy groan like a dying man. "I know this isn't the greatest time to say this, but this is why you shouldn't try to deal with your shoulder on your own."

"I know, I know. Damn shoulder is why I never got a shot at playing pro."

"You'll be fine in a few weeks. This next week, you need to keep that arm in a sling. No exceptions." The doctor narrows her eyes at Jimmy. "You remember what happened last time you didn't follow my orders, right?"

Jimmy looks sheepish as he looks up at the pretty doctor. This is obviously not the first time she's set Jimmy's shoulder for him. If she is who I think she is, she's the one that nearly put him in a hard cast after he played a game when his shoulder wasn't healed and he came back less than a week after she had set it.

"Yes, ma'am. Don't worry. I know I'm not getting any younger. Besides," he grins, his eyes starting to sparkle from the effects of the painkiller they gave him, "I can get these two here to do the Christmas cooking. That'll be fun to watch."

"What?" Mandy's voice rises to a shrill pitch that makes everyone wince. "I can handle all the cooking just fine."

"Tell that to the ham you scorched three years ago."

Mandy grumbles and looks away from Jimmy, embarrassment coloring her cheeks.

"I like to cook, though I'm not always the most attentive… and sometimes things get burnt." Mandy doesn't look me in the eye as she says this and it takes all my self-control to not smile. In high school, she always had this persona of having everything together and being in control, even though I knew from Jimmy that that wasn't really the case.

"Trevor, man. Make sure she doesn't kill the ham. It's not Christmas without ham. Don't kill the ham. Please?" Jimmy's eyes are drooping and whatever they gave him for the pain is kicking in strong.

"Can *you* even cook?" Mandy challenges me, her eyes narrowed and highly skeptical.

I step closer to Mandy, my eyes locked on hers. "I know how to do more with my hands than just throw a football."

The blush that flames across her face makes me smile and makes my cock vibrate with desire. I'm gonna have permanent blue balls if I can't get her alone and naked sometime soon. I need to be close to her, because I need to know if she feels the way I do.

Mandy eventually cuts her eyes away and it thrills me to see just how flustered she is.

"Okay. Fine. Let's take Jimmy home, then you can buy me that beer and tell me about these supposed mad cooking skills you have."

"Deal."

~

"AND THAT," I push a paper coaster with a dinner menu listed on it toward Mandy, "is how I think we should do Christmas dinner."

Mandy looks at me, then looks back down at the menu. She lets out a low whistle and shakes her head. Her auburn hair falls in her face and I instinctively push it behind her ear.

"Oh!" Mandy jumps like she's been electrocuted. Even though she's not saying a word, she's studying me closely, a million emotions and thoughts racing across her pretty face.

Seeing Mandy squirm makes me want her even more. Little by little, her tough girl façade is cracking. I know she wants me, but I know I also have to work for it. One bad play and she'll be saying no to me for the million and tenth time.

"Are you okay?" I turn my bar stool so I'm facing her and put my hand on her knee. Her eyes follow my hand and my heart isn't the only thing pounding when she puts her hand on mine.

"Oh, I think I'm quite okay. Don't you?" She smiles at me, her cheeks red from the beer and the heat of the bar.

"I think you're more than okay," I say, leaning closer toward her. Something has shifted in her, whether the beer or something else, but no way in hell am I going to ask her what changed – I'm just thankful that she's opening herself up to me. I curve my hand so that it's on the back of her knee, then I pull her knee out so that I can stand up in front of her, between her legs. "In fact, I think you're quite spectacular."

"You don't say, Trevor?"

I see the smile on her lips and know that I'm a goner. Her lips are full and perfect.

"I've been saying this for years. Or don't you remember?"

"Maybe I need a little reminding. Perhaps—"

"OH MY GOD! Trevor Collins! Is that really you?"

I take a deep breath and turn my head toward a shrill voice I recognize. Jessica Yarrow.

Fuck.

"Jessie. How ya been?"

I watch Jessie look at me, then at Mandy, then to my hand on Mandy's knee. Jessie's forehead creases and she tilts her head.

"I'm well. Why don't you come over, talk with me a few minutes?" Jessie bats her eyes. That used to mean something to me, in high school, but it doesn't phase me anymore. "You don't mind, do you Mindy?"

"It's Mandy." Mandy's voice is tight.

"No thank you," I say, aggravated at how Jessie flicks her blonde hair and turns so that she's facing me, and aggressively ignoring Mandy.

"Come on over, please? You can join us, too, Mandy."

"No. We were just leaving, weren't we Mandy?"

Mandy looks at me, confusion and upset on her face. My parents raised me to be polite, but I will be rude to Jessie if I need to. I'm here with Mandy and she's the only person important to me right now.

"Sorry about that," I say once we're in the parking lot and away from the bar. "Let's go somewhere else."

"No, that's okay. I'm going to head home." The sadness in her voice kills me. I'd do anything to make this right, but reading her body language doesn't take a pro football player to read. She's glancing toward her car and the sexy vibe we had going is gone. Fuck.

CHAPTER 5

MANDY

"How's your brother doing?" Grace asks as she parks her car in the crowded mall parking lot. We're on a mission for toys for her nephew.

I roll my eyes at Grace.

"That bad, huh?"

"I'll let you guess," I sigh. "He's not doing anything big…yet, but that's just a matter of time. I love my brother, but he has no idea when to slow down. I'm scared that one day he won't be able to bounce back fully."

"Men." Grace shakes her head, a rueful smile on her face.

"Brothers!"

"Oh, speaking of men," Grace grins, threading her arm through mine as we navigate through cars and families in the parking lot. "Do tell about you and Trevor. That tackle of yours was…let's just say you were heating up the whole city there for a minute!"

I can't help from smiling at the memory of Trevor. The feeling of his ripped body beneath mine was fantastic.

"My God he's hot."

"Hot, and totally and only has eyes for you, babe. What happened with you two after you took your brother to the hospital?"

The memory of last night at the bar wipes the smile off my face. Grace looks at me when I don't immediately respond and her smile falters.

"Uh oh. What happened? Because by the look on your face, what everyone *thought* was going to happen clearly didn't."

"Yeah, no. I slept alone last night." I tug my scarf so that it fits more snugly around my neck, then pull Grace faster toward the mall. "Let's get inside. It's cold out here."

"Uh oh. What happened?"

I tell Grace about the flirting and how it ignited something in me, something more than just lust, and how I really, really wanted to sleep with him, but how Jessie showed up and killed the mood.

"Wait. You were going to go home with him? You always pushed him away, in high school. Not to mention you're just out of a relationship…"

"Yes, you're right on both points. But it just felt different, you know?" I point at a truck set, but Grace shakes her head and we keep moving down the toy aisle. "There was something more between us, more than just sexual fizz. We may live in different cities, but…I don't know. Maybe I was hoping for something more."

Grace turns and laughs at me, her face breaking into a smile as she starts laughing.

"What?"

"*Maybe.* Girl, you should hear yourself. There was no maybe in your voice. Something has been brewing between the two of you for *years.* I thought maybe it would finally happen with you two – and I'm not just talking about banging hot sex!"

A grandmother looks at us and I mouth *sorry*. To Grace, I say, "Keep your voice down. We don't need everyone knowing about my failed shot with Trevor."

"Sorry," Grace says. "What do you think of this?" She points at a mini foosball set.

"That looks like fun. Is he old enough for that?"

"Yeah." Grace grabs the big box and we head for the front of the store and the cashiers. "But what about you? Are you going to be okay? Are you going to see him again?"

This time, it's my turn to start laughing. "Oh, Grace. I didn't tell you about what happened at the hospital."

"Oh, no. I thought everything was okay?"

"What? Oh, Jimmy will be fine, as long as he follows the doctor's orders. I mean more like Jimmy can't cook Christmas dinner like he's been planning."

"God, I hadn't even thought of that. What are you going to do? Are you just going to go out? Get some catering in?"

"Well, if only it was that easy!" I laugh again, enjoying how it feels. "No. Jimmy immediately said that dinner is on Trevor and me."

"What?!"

"Exactly. Last night, he even came up with an amazing menu plan. I think he really does know how to cook."

"That's good, because…" Grace looks at me, the apology in her eyes.

"Yeah, yeah. I know. I'm not Susie Homemaker when it comes to cooking, alright?"

Grace shakes her head and lets out a low whistle. "Are you going to be okay with that? You're not going to be able to escape seeing him. If it was me, that would be awkward as hell…"

"Tell me about it. But I don't see another option. I'm certainly not going to abandon my brother on Christmas and certainly not when his arm is messed up and he has to take it easy."

The idea of Trevor Collins, star quarterback for the Austin Blues, in a kitchen with an apron on? Oh yeah, that's hot. H-O-T. I've always dreamt of having a boyfriend who cooked for me, which sadly has so far been nothing but a dream.

"I'll do what I can to help, you know. Not sure I can do anything, but even if it's just faking an emergency that needs your help, I've got your back." Grace gives me a hug as we wait in the check-out line.

"You're the best," I whisper to her, emotions rising in me. A lot of the time, it feels like I'm lost, like I should have figured out life already.

"No, you are…even if you can't cook to save your life."

I smile and hug her tighter.

"My cooking isn't that bad!"

~

"Hey, sis. How ya doin'?"

Jimmy's laid out on the couch, one arm in a sling and another holding on to a bottle of beer.

"Doing alright." I kick off my shoes and go to the end of the couch, making him move his feet. "How's your shoulder feeling? Are you really supposed to be drinking beer with those painkillers?"

I love my brother, and as an EMT he should know better, but sometimes he's foolish.

When Jimmy mutes the game he's watching, I know something serious is up. I offer up a quick prayer that he hasn't had bad news from the doctor.

"So. Mandy. What's going on with you and Trevor?"

I freeze. I've never really been comfortable talking about guys with my brother, and I'm not sure I want to start now – especially about Trevor.

"Uh…nothing. Nothing is happening."

"Sis, don't try to lie to me. There's been something between you two since high school. You looked ready to hump him on the field yesterday. But today, you've been smiling, but I can tell you're not happy. What's wrong? Do I need to go teach Trevor a thing or two about messing with my sister?"

"You couldn't throw a half-decent punch if your life depended on it," I laugh, pointedly looking at his injured arm.

Jimmy looks at his sling and laughs with me.

"In any case, nothing is going on. Honestly." I'm not going to tell my brother about how Trevor was touching my leg last night or how I was ready, as he so eloquently put it, hump the living daylights out of him.

"I'm not sure I believe you," Jimmy finally says, giving me a long look. "You gonna be okay with him around and helping him with Christmas dinner? Just because I can't cook doesn't mean Christmas dinner is off."

This has been the thing I've thought about most of the day. Can I face Trevor after last night? Do I even want to? I wasn't lying when I told Grace that I can't and won't abandon my brother. That's not what family does, and my brother is more important than whatever is, or *isn't*, going on between me and Trevor.

I take a deep breath and nod my head. "Yeah, I'll be fine."

"Good. Because he's on his way over, so you can go do the shopping for the dinner."

CHAPTER 6

TREVOR

"Hi, Trevor." Mandy's voice is tight when she greets me at the door and it's obvious something is wrong.

Inside, it's obvious that there's something going on with her brother, though he's grinning.

"So, you're here to take me grocery shopping?" Mandy says, pulling on her coat. "Let's get it over with."

I look at Jimmy, but he keeps on smiling and shrugs, in a *don't argue, man, just do it* way. Taking on three-hundred-pound guys on the field is easy compared to being around a woman who's upset.

"Yeah, I thought we could try and get a jump on the crowds. Seems Jimmy, here," I smile, trying to inject some levity in the room, "did not stock up before blowing out his shoulder."

Mandy glares at Jimmy, who's stretched out on the couch, beer in one hand and remote control resting on his stomach.

"Don't blame me. I don't mind all the crowds."

Something that sounds a lot like *whatever* comes from Mandy, then she's quickly walking to the door.

I pause when we get outside. "You want to drive?"

Right now, the main goal is to find out what's going on and to try fix whatever is wrong.

"Yeah, I'll drive. Get in."

Mandy doesn't speak until we get to the grocery store.

"Look. I'll admit I need help cooking Christmas dinner. But let's just stay out of each other's way, okay?"

"Mandy, what's wrong?" The vibes she's sending off are explosive. Whatever is under her skin is deeply under her skin.

"What?" Mandy looks at me and pauses, the look on her face softening just a little. "No, it's fine. I just wasn't expecting… any of this. It's been a hard month. I'll be fine."

"You sure?" She doesn't look fine and knowing her, I don't believe that she will be anytime soon.

"Yeah. Let's get going."

"ALRIGHT. That's everything from my list," I say, doublechecking the mountain of food in the cart. "Is there anything else you need? Might as well stock up since we're here."

"Um, yeah. Hold on. Why don't you get in line?"

"Sure thing."

I maneuver toward the snaking lines by the cashiers and let myself feel a little bit of hope. Mandy's discomfort thawed a little as we shopped and I *think* this won't be the most awkward thing I've ever done.

It takes longer than a minute for Mandy to return and when she does, her arms are loaded down with boxes and bags of fruit.

"Why didn't you grab a basket?" I ask, shaking my head as I help her put everything in the cart.

"I didn't think I would see so much I wanted or that Jimmy probably needs." There's a sweet *oof* to her voice as she drops the last of her last-minute shopping in the cart. It warms my heart that even though she was upset with her brother when I picked her up, she's still thinking of him and showing how she cares by making sure he has what he needs.

I'm grateful when we make it through the cashier's line and out to the parking lot without people coming up to talk to me. I don't mind talking to fans, but all I want right now is to be with Mandy, without being interrupted. I need her to know that she comes first.

I put all the groceries in the trunk while Mandy warms up the car.

"Okay. That's done." I close the door behind me, grateful for the warmth of the car.

Mandy's doesn't notice as I pull something special out of my pocket.

"Hey. Hold up a sec. There's something else."

Mandy's sigh is irritated and she turns the car off. "What now?"

I pull the mistletoe I bought out of my pocket and place it above our heads.

"This."

I pull Mandy into a kiss and an erotic charge goes straight to my groin. For a moment, her body is tense, but then her body melts against mine. Her lips are soft and sweet, and I have to restrain myself from just devouring her. Yet when she opens her mouth and her delicious little tongue darts out and touches mine, I let myself go. Weaving my fingers through her silky auburn hair, I hold her tightly and plunge my tongue deeper into her mouth. Mandy moans and kisses me back fiercely.

It feels like being a teenager again, making out in a car. This is exactly how I wish it had been between us in high school, if only I hadn't been such an idiot and scared of her brother. I haven't felt awkward about a woman in a very long time. Though when the woman is your best friend's little sister, you can't help but be nervous.

I lower one of my hands to inside of her coat and she pushes her breast into my hand. Even her thick sweater can't hide how exquisitely hard her nipple is under my fingers.

"We should—"

A sharp honking interrupts us and we look up to see a driver glaring at us, aggressively motioning in a "get out or get moving because I want your parking spot" way.

"We should get home, yes." Mandy's voice and hands tremble.

As I put my hand on hers as she starts the car, the smile she gives me lets me know it was worth it to her, too.

This is going to be the best Christmas ever.

CHAPTER 7

MANDY

"What was that?" My voice warbles as I try to catch my breath, my heart thumping like it's going to burst out of my chest.

Trevor's smile is slow and gorgeous across his mouth. "That, Mandy, was a kiss in the tradition of Christmas and mistletoe."

"That was not just a friendly Christmas kiss," I protest. I don't know what's going on. I liked the kiss. No, I *loved* the kiss. But how is he attracted to me? We're not in high school anymore and I'm definitely not the kind of woman he dates – I've seen all the pictures online of his girlfriends. There's this weird push-pull going on between us and it's confusing as hell.

But kissing him… It filled my heart and soul with happiness. It was a kiss with more than passion – it held *promise*. I was expecting *fun,* not something that…not a kiss that felt more meaningful than any kiss I've ever had.

"No, it wasn't." Trevor leans toward me again, brushing my hair from my face. "You're the one that got away, Mandy."

I'm glad the car isn't in motion, because I'm pretty certain I'd swerve into oncoming traffic about now. All I can do is stare at him. The look in Trevor's eyes is earnest, not like he's teasing me. Is this really happening? Is something with Trevor even remotely possible? But of course not, it's not like he lives here, and my life will be once it's February and I can finally leave my job and move home.

Trevor pulls back, as much as his muscle-bound body can in my small car. "Can you say something? Am I out of line?"

"No," I say, once I can actually speak again. "It's just…you know. I'd thought we'd have a bit of fun," I say, inwardly wincing at the white lie, but scared to admit that I've been hoping for more, "and that we'd go back to our normal lives in a few days. You've just made it serious."

"Mandy, I *am* serious." Trevor reaches out and puts his hand on mine.

I flinch, not believing what he's saying. I'm famously bad at choosing men to date, so it's hard to believe it would be any different with Trevor. Trevor Collins! We strung each other along in high school and I can't believe that he's not doing the same thing now. Sure, everything *feels* different, but I can't believe that it *is* different.

"I… I don't know." Trevor looks serious, but… Can I really believe him? "I need to get these groceries home and in the refrigerator. I'll drop you off on the way home."

Out of the corner of my eye, I see Trevor nod and slump back in his seat.

I grip the steering wheel tightly, wishing I could go back to the touch football game and take back tackling Trevor. All of this started because of that and I didn't even mean to do it.

~

"WHEN WILL I EVER LEARN?" I hate the whine in my voice, but I can't help it.

"I don't know…" Grace says, leaning back in her chair, her hands wrapped around a grande hot chocolate.

"I mean, he looked serious. That kiss was *definitely* serious. But… come *on*. After all this time? The guy who got away is actually interested in me? A *pro football player* is interested in me? That doesn't happen to girls like me!"

My voice goes shrill and I slap my hand over my mouth when I see people at the next table looking over at us. It's not like I need my problems to be broadcast.

"You're not going to like this, but I'm still going to say it, Mandy. You need to talk to Trevor," Grace says, seriously. "You two have been circling each other since high school. I don't know how you think you could just hook up with him for a night, maybe two, and have that be it."

"But…"

"Mandy, look at me. There are no buts about it. There are too many emotions and too much history between you two."

I slump in my seat, briefly cursing the Christmas music. *All I Want For Christmas Is You* comes on and all I want for Christmas is to hide from the world or at least live in a universe where I didn't feel bad for being single. I want Trevor so bad, but I know it would never work. If we didn't figure things out in high school, how can I expect that we could work things out *now*?

"I don't know..."

"Mandy, I know and I know you do, too. I know it's scary, but you have to face it. You'll never know, otherwise."

"But what if everything goes south, like with every other guy I've liked or dated? Why should I believe Trevor is any different?"

"Relationships are mysterious. The thing is, you don't and can't know. You just have to take the chance and put your heart out there."

"I know, I know. It's just my heart is bruised, you know? I don't have faith in myself." I look away from Grace, unable to meet her eyes. There are tears pricking at my eyes and I know that if I see sympathy from Grace, it will push me over the edge.

"Oh, sweetie. You're an amazing woman. You're smart and talented and beautiful. Any man that doesn't recognize that is an abject fool."

I smile at Grace and wipe tears from the corners of my eyes. "You're making me cry."

"I'm ready to cry if you're going to give up. Don't give up."

"I'll try." I take a deep breath, trying to calm my emotions. If there's one thing the holidays are good for, it's an abundance of emotions.

"One last thing. Despite how Trevor was in high school, he is not an abject fool."

CHAPTER 8

TREVOR

Reginald, bro. I'm sorry, but I'm out. I've already talked to Coach Freeman. I don't want to be crippled for life – and if I keep playing, my knee is going to go out and that's exactly what's going to happen. It's not public yet, but I'm retiring. It's not a publicity stunt, not like Josiah pulled two years ago."

"Man… We need our captain back. You're the glue that holds us together. We're getting our asses handed to us. Even the Royals beat us this year." I can hear the frustration and disappointment in my former teammate's voice. The Austin Blues have been hurting this year, since our old coach packed up and went to another team.

"I'm sorry you guys have it rough this year, really. But I'm not kidding about retiring."

Reginald's laugh is sharp and fast. "You seriously think you're going to be happy with life in a small town? I can keep the door open a little while longer, but don't wait too long…"

"You know the flashy lifestyle was never really for me. Not saying it's not fun and seductive, but it's not a long-term thing for me. Coaching high school football is where my future is – my school was great when I was there and I want to take them to state again, this time as their coach. I want to give back to the school that gave me my start."

"You're a better man than I am, Trevor. Look, I gotta run. Esme's nearly here and we have to bust ass to get out to her mom's."

"Yeah, I gotta jet, too. I got a Christmas ham to bake."

"Dude. You're *cooking*? What's her name?"

I smile as I think of Mandy. It's useless to pretend I don't love my best friend's sister.

"Mandy. And it's for her brother, too. Idiot dislocated his shoulder. I'm just the fill-in cook."

"Don't try to downplay it. I know how you are about cooking – you don't just do that for anyone. You only cook for family. They must be important."

"True. I've known Mandy and Jimmy since I was six."

Reginald's deep voice booms in laughter, and then he lets out a long, low whistle.

"This is the girl that got away, isn't it? Don't think I've forgotten you mentioning her."

"Yeah, that's her. Not sure how it's going, because everything stops before it starts or she's mad at me."

"The madder she is, the more she cares. Look at me and Esme."

I laugh. Reginald's wife is a spitfire. At barely five feet, she has Reginald and all two-hundred-sixty pounds of his muscle under control. Reginald may be one of the superstars of the Austin Blues, but she leads their marriage.

"Yeah, something tells me Mandy and Esme would get on like a house on fire."

A car horn bleats three times and I can hear Reginald huffing as he walks through the winter air.

"Look. You figure it out. You've won three Superbowl rings – you can figure out the plays for this girl. I'll bet my ring on it."

I sure hope so. I'm ready to bet everything on Mandy.

"As much as you may think I'm a dumb jock, let me show you what I can do in the kitchen."

I turn and smile at Mandy, but she's leaning against the back door, arms across her deliciously plump chest, her eyebrow raised at me.

"I don't know how you think you can cook better than I can," she finally says, going to the sink and washing her hands, then pushing up her sleeves. My eyes lock on her full breasts and how they shift under the thin fabric of her blouse as she pulls her hair up into a bun.

"Mandy, you know I adore you," I raise my eyes and focus on her brilliant blue eyes. "But you can't cook and we know it. Everyone knows it."

Mandy's cheeks color, but she doesn't look away.

"Doesn't mean I can't learn." Her voice is defensive, but she's not retreating. *Good.* I can work with this. I love that she's willing to try and learn, instead of doubling down in stubbornness.

"I'm glad to hear that. What we're going to do isn't too complicated, not like French cooking, but we do have to get it right."

"Uh huh."

I watch her eyes rake up and down my body, lingering over the apron I've wrapped around my waist. "Do you want an apron? It'll protect that pretty blouse of yours." Though if she got something on her blouse and I had to take it off…

Mandy makes short work of chopping the vegetables I stack in front of her. The carrot matchsticks are a little uneven, but it doesn't matter at all.

Wiping my hands on my apron, I go to the fridge and pull out some potatoes.

"Okay. These need to be peeled and then sliced into rounds. Sound good?"

"Sure."

I slice up several onions, then turn my attention back to Mandy. She's focused on the potatoes and she's doing an excellent job. My guess is that she's just never cooked much, not that she has no skill for cooking.

"All done," she says, looking up at me, a smile on her face.

"Those are perfect." This is not a lie. The more she helps me, the more I see her relaxing and looking confident. "Now let's trim up some more of the vegetables, and then—"

Mandy's forehead creases as she interrupts me. "What's with all the vegetables? Was buying meat a diversion? Are you secretly a *vegetarian?*"

"Oh, Mandy. Honey. No." I laugh loudly, wiping my eyes and then instantly regretting it as tears stream from my eyes, thanks to onion juice I forgot to wash from my hands.

"I didn't think it was that funny."

I squint at Mandy and I can see she's closing in on herself again.

"I'm sorry. I didn't mean to make you uncomfortable. I couldn't maintain this," I say, gesturing down toward my body, puffing out my chest a little when Mandy's eyes follow my hands and linger on my body, "if I didn't eat meat. You'd be hard-pressed to find a vegetarian football player – one, the guys just aren't like that; and two, it would be too hard to get all the protein we need."

"Thanks." Mandy's smile is thin, but at least she's still here. "I suppose I see what you're saying."

"Alright. Let's get everything ready for the salad, and then we should be good to go. The rest we can take care of in the morning."

I move to where Mandy is at the counter and stand beside her, and we both start chopping. I have her chopping bread into squares, to bake into croutons.

God. This is what I want, right here. Mandy and I, side by side, working and living and loving together.

A familiar twitch and tightening hits my groin and I cough.

"That's it for now. Beer?"

"That sounds amazing. Yes, please."

I grab two beers from the fridge, then we head into the living room. For once, I'm glad that Jimmy isn't here, but upstairs resting.

"What was this talk of you moving home?" I ask as I watch Mandy settle onto the opposite end of the couch. A primal instinct has me wanting to reach out and pull her close to me, but I know that would be the wrong move with her.

Mandy sighs and peels the edge of the label on the beer bottle she's holding.

"It's been tough in Seattle. I miss my friends here and I miss my brother. It's going to sound quaint, so don't laugh," she says, giving me a long, narrow-eyed look of warning, "but I miss life in a smaller town. I want a family of my own and I'm not sure I want to do that in Seattle. I don't want to have to worry about my kids going outside to play."

"I know what you mean," I say, taking a long drink of my beer. "I've wanted to move home for a long time, too."

Mandy's laugh is full and rich, and it makes me want to make her laugh every hour of every day.

"Yeah, right. You're just trying to charm me again. I don't believe a word of it." The smile Mandy gives me, full of playfulness and affection, it goes straight to my heart. "Who would give up the career that you fought so hard for? I remember how you worked your ass off in high school. Playing pro ball isn't something someone just gives up."

"Maybe I am trying to charm you…" I say, ignoring the fact that she's wrong. I'm leaving the Blues and coming home. I move closer to her on the couch and smile when she shivers as I run my fingers down her arm. "Maybe I'm trying to match your flirting game."

"What flirting game?" Mandy asks, her voice suddenly quieter and breathless.

I move my hand across her wrist and take her hand in mine, pulling her closer to me. She doesn't resist.

"The flirting game of tackling me the other day." She's now so close I can feel her breath puffing against my mouth. My mouth presses against her plump lips and her body presses against mine, her hand tentatively wrapping around my neck. Kissing her again is fan-fucking-tastic. Teasing her, I pull back from our kiss. "The flirting game that you started in middle school." I kiss her again, my tongue teasing her. The taste of beer lingers on her lips and it's indescribable how good she tastes and how much I want to drink Mandy and her kiss in.

"I'm not…sure…" Mandy blinks her eyes rapidly, her fingers pushing up into my hair. "I'm pretty sure it was you who teased me back then."

"Are you sure about that?" I lower my mouth to her neck and scrape her skin with my teeth, before sucking at her neck and making her moan.

"Oh my… And what… what about the mistletoe?" Mandy groans and I can feel her body heat burning against my body.

"What about," I lick her neck slowly, "the mistletoe?" I kiss her along her jaw and she leans into me. I drop a hand down to her chest and slowly caress her breasts, and discover her nipples poking urgently against my fingertips.

"That…was you…teasing…me."

I snake my arm around her waist and urge her even closer. Mandy moves so that she's straddling my lap and every fiber of my being is loudly demanding to strip off her clothes and make love to her all night long. Tonight, and every night to come.

Mandy's blue eyes meet mine, then she cups her soft hands along my jaw and lowers her mouth to mine. She nips at my lips, then parts my lips with her tongue, and then I'm falling into her and falling into how good she feels, how right Mandy feels. My hands roam her body, loving the feel of her soft curves, the weight of her on top of me.

Wrapping my hands around her ass, I bless whomever made leggings, because I can feel her ass clearly and I'm already fantasizing about bending her over and losing myself inside of her. If just kissing and groping her feels like this, burying my cock deep inside of Mandy is going to make me lose my mind in the best possible way.

"I think we need," Mandy nips at my earlobe, "go somewhere more—"

We both freeze as heavy footsteps echo as Jimmy walks down the stairs from his bedroom. In a scene that feels like it's out of a high school playbook, Mandy leaps off my lap and frantically smooths her hair and clothes, looking around wildly like her parents are about to walk in and discover us. I try and hide the raging hard-on pressing against my jeans, quickly grabbing a throw blanket to spread across my lap.

Like that is going to fool anyone, especially Jimmy...

Jimmy turns the corner from the stairs and looks at us, one arm in a sling and the other hand wiping his face.

"Man, I didn't expect to sleep so long. What've you two been up to?"

CHAPTER 9

MANDY

Cheers!" Jimmy, Grace, Trevor, and I all clink glasses once everyone has loaded up their plates with the meal Trevor and I cooked today. For as much as I *don't* know about cooking, I have to admit I had fun with Trevor in the kitchen. He made everything seem interesting and not-intimidating. It made me want to spend more time in the kitchen and learn how to cook better.

With his fork halfway to his mouth, Jimmy looks from Trevor to me, then back to Trevor.

"Trevor, I think we all need to know – what did you cook and what did Mandy cook?" His eyes glitter with laughter.

"Hey! I resent that!" I exclaim, though I'm laughing. I load up my fork with scalloped potatoes and I groan with genuine pleasure when I taste it.

"Well, I guess we know what dish Mandy made," Jimmy says, eyeing the scalloped potatoes warily.

"It was entirely a joint effort," Trevor says, a megawatt smile on his lips. "Mandy was a joy to cook with. I don't know why you all don't think she can cook."

Grace coughs, then stares at Jimmy, her eyes open.

"Trevor? Is there rum in the eggnog you've been drinking? Haven't you heard about Mandy's cooking? I know you two haven't seen each other in a while, but… Mandy is kind of legendary."

"You guys," I groan, rolling my eyes. "I'm not that bad!"

"Yes, you are!" Jimmy and Grace chime in unison.

"Well, be that as it may," Trevor says, pausing to take a bite of food. "I did lead the cooking, yes. That doesn't mean Mandy couldn't hold her own in the kitchen. And everything truly was a joint effort."

"You'll never get a husband if you can't cook," Jimmy teases, taking the joke too far.

"Or maybe I just need a husband who cooks. Who says it's still the woman's role to do all the cooking?" I try to keep my voice light and do my damnedest to keep my emotions in check, but my brother's dig hurts – and he knows it.

"Oh, come on!" I slap the counter of the bar and shake my head in disbelief as I watch the game on the big screen TV. I take a long drink of my beer and cover my mouth at the burp that rises up. "How did the ref miss that interference?"

The other guys at the bar and the bartender all look at me and nod sadly. The refs this game have it in for us. This isn't their first bad call.

"They're sure making it hard for us to get to post-season," the guy on my left says.

"Oh, don't be so hasty. That wasn't an interference and the call was good."

I swear under my breath at the voice coming from my right, even before I turn and see his face.

"What are you doing here?" I turn and ask Trevor. I'm still upset about what happened at dinner, even if it wasn't his fault. I left because I needed space, not to be tracked down.

"Looking for you, as it happens. You left rather abruptly, you might remember."

I grab my beer tightly and look away from Trevor. As soon as dinner was over, I excused myself to come out for a beer, alone. I thought I'd been graceful about it, but maybe not.

"It's just...the holidays are hard. I hate that the first question everyone asks is if I have a boyfriend or a fiancé. And yes, I get that my cooking skills are...rudimentary, but maybe people could let up a bit." I admit, hearing the tightness in my voice. A couple of beers hasn't been enough to help me relax. Right now, I'm just down on the holidays. No boyfriend. Mad at my brother. "I'm going to head home tomorrow."

"Do you have to go back to work so soon?"

"Not really, no," I say, waving to the bartender for another beer. I hold two fingers up. Might as well get one for Trevor, since he doesn't look like he's just passing through. "It's just...I had a bad breakup recently. I was hoping to escape that over the holidays. That's all."

"I understand," Trevor says, quickly moving onto the newly empty barstool beside me.

"You have got to be kidding, right? You must have more girl-friends than you can even manage." The words come out of my mouth sour and jealous, and I immediately regret it. "Sorry," I add quickly. "It's just…hard night and big feelings."

Trevor gives me a long look, then takes a long drink of his beer.

"Anyway," I say, wrapping my fingers around my beer bottle to stop them from shaking. What was I thinking, admitting this to Trevor? "Anyway, did Jimmy send you here to be all cagey, to lure me back to the house?" I ask, keeping Trevor in my line of sight as I watch the game. We're halfway through the third quarter, ball in hand and we're in the middle of a big drive. A touchdown is looking imminent.

"No," he says, a slow smile spreading across his mouth. "I came for you. Me. The only agenda is mine."

My insides flutter and somersault as I listen to Trevor. Our unfinished business washes over me and before I even realize what I'm doing, my fingers are on his wrist and stroking that spot where the base of his thumb meets his wrist.

"That's a dangerous thing you're doing there," Trevor says, but he doesn't pull away. The rest of the bar cheers as our team makes a touchdown, but Trevor and I keep staring at each other, the electricity building up all over again.

"Maybe a girl needs a little danger in her life? Why don't we just have some fun. You're leaving soon and I'm—"

"Hold up," Trevor says, putting a finger on my lips. "I'm actually not leaving. I'm back to stay."

I blink rapidly, wrapping my mind around the words I'm pretty sure he just said. I haven't had so much beer that I'm hallucinating, have I?

"I… What?"

"I've been offered a job coaching at the high school. Coach Fitzgerald is retiring in June." Trevor pauses, not once looking away from me. "I've already accepted the job. We're both coming back home, Mandy."

"Oh," I mumble, unable to say anything coherent.

The universe has a funny way of doing things. I thought coming home would give me a break from the heartache I've felt, but now? Now I'm going to see Trevor regularly? That makes my heart ache in a different, more painful way. I honestly don't know if I can take seeing him around, eventually settling down with another woman. It would feel like just another man that I've loved, but who didn't love me back.

"Mandy, why do you look so blue? I thought you would be happy to hear this," Trevor says, leaning closer to me. "Jimmy telling me that you were moving home is the reason I agreed to the job."

CHAPTER 10

TREVOR

“Excuse me, what?” Mandy's head snaps toward me, her eyes blazing.

"When I heard that you're moving back here," I say, reaching out and putting my hand over hers, "that sealed the deal for me. Coach Fitzgerald has been after me to take his job for months now. When he heard I was retiring, he started campaigning to get me to take over."

"But..." Mandy's mouth open and closes. Her eyes are bright and I can see her mind racing, even though her mouth keeps opening and closing, and no words come out. "Would you really be happy here?"

"Why wouldn't I be happy here? Everything I need to make me happy is here. *You're* here." I squeeze her hands with mine and gently caress them. Her body tenses a little bit, but she doesn't pull her hands away.

"Won't you miss playing with your team? Going from professional sports to be a high school coach, that's a really big change. What about the fame and flashy lifestyle?"

"Of course I'll miss playing with the team. They've become my brothers. We're a family. They mean the world to me, but pro ball isn't the life I want. My knee can't take much more damage, anyway. Worrying about hurting it keeps me from playing like I want to play and how my team needs me to play."

Mandy's eyes narrow and I get the distinct sense that she doesn't believe me about any of this.

"But is it going to be enough, to be back here?"

"Mandy," I say, pulling her hands so that she's standing in front of me, between my legs. "Look, sure. Fame is fun. But it gets old. Believe me when I say it's not a line that I want to settle down, too." I look into Mandy's eyes and her body stills. "It's why I'm moving back home. You were the one who got away. Now's my chance to fix that."

I stand up and wrap my arms around Mandy, pulling her into a kiss. I have every intention of going slow, enjoy this moment…but when she wraps her arms around me and pulls me tightly against her soft curves, I can't help myself. My tongue pushes hard at her lips, desperate to taste her again. She needs a reason to believe I'm staying and I want my kiss to show her just how serious I am.

Mandy moans into my mouth and deepens our kiss, and I pull her closer, desperate for there to be no space between us.

A loud ruckus around us catches my attention and we both pull apart, panting as we stare into each other's eyes.

"Did we score?" Mandy asks, glancing toward the TV. But all that's on is a beer commercial.

"I think so." I don't give a fuck about the game on the TV. All I care about is Mandy and doing what we've needed to do for years. I let my fingers caress her waist, my heart pounding that this is finally happening. "I don't care, Mandy. I care about you. Let's get out of here."

CHAPTER 11

MANDY

Trevor and I practically fall over ourselves as we leave the bar. The air has changed between us. The flirting we did during the football game, that pales compared to the electricity between us now. This attraction, it's not about having fun – there's nothing casual about the way we're looking at each other or talking to each other. Everything contains the gravity of commitment.

"I always wanted you. Fuck. I wanted you so bad in high school, but your brother would have massacred me."

I grin at Trevor and squeezes his hand tighter in mine. The pent-up desire I've had for Trevor unlocks within me and fills the very essence of my being.

"I wanted you, too, but you were too popular. Jimmy warned me about you, too. He said you were no good and that you'd break my heart."

Trevor's laugh echoes down the streets and a dog barks in the distance.

"That sure sounds like Jimmy. But to be fair, he was probably right. I didn't know what I was doing back then and I probably *would* have broken your heart. Even though I've dreamed about you for so long, I'm glad that this is happening now. I'm not scared of what I want. I'm the man I've always wanted to be."

"Are you sure?" I ask, needing reassurance. I'm happier than I've ever been, but there's a little voice inside my head that's telling me it's not going to work out. It's never worked out with other guys before, so why should I think it will now?

But this is Trevor. I know Trevor and he knows me. This isn't just some random flirtation.

Trevor stops walking and holds me so that I stop walking, too.

"Mandy," his voice quiets as he pulls me closer to him. "You are the one I've always wanted, too. It's never worked out with anybody else, because they weren't you."

"I think that's why it's never worked out for me, with anyone else, either," I whisper, pressing my body against Trevor's. "This is just scary, you know? I've dreamed about you for so long, too, that it almost doesn't seem real that this is really happening. I want it to happen and I truly love you."

"Then let me show you how much I love you, too." Trevor pushes my hair back from my face and holds my jaw gently as he lowers his mouth to mine, then gives me the slowest and most intimate kiss ever.

Our tongues dance slowly as we stand on the sidewalk. An urgency grows in our kiss, but it's not the raw urgency of lust, but an urgency to do what we wanted to do for so long to seal our love for each other.

"Oh my God! It's about time you two hooked up!" Grace's voice calls from across the street.

Trevor and I bump heads as I jump at the sound of Grace's voice.

Trevor hugs me tightly as Grace crosses the snowy street to meet us. Snow is starting to fall again and I'm grinning like an idiot.

"I'm working on a long-term arrangement," Trevor calls out, tightening his arms around me. My insides quiver with nerves and excitement. I can't believe this is really happening.

Grace narrows her eyes at Trevor when she finally makes it over to us.

"Trevor Collins," she says, her voice stern. "If you string my best friend along, you will have *me* to answer to," she pokes Trevor in the chest and glares at him, "and I will make your life miserable. Are we clear?"

"Yes, ma'am," he says, smiling. "I want nothing but to make her happy. You're a fierce friend. I respect that."

"Good. You okay?" She turns to me and her face softens. "I'm really happy for you. No one deserves happiness more than you do."

"Tonight's turning out alright," I say, laughing and holding Trevor's body tightly. His body is so strong and so warm, and I can't wait to be somewhere private with him so that we can make love. Finally.

"Good! I'm really happy for both of you."

"This is better than winning a Super Bowl ring. Now if you'll excuse us, I need to take Mandy home."

My stomach flip flops with anticipation and happiness. Grace gives me a quick hug, and then Trevor and I make our way to his hotel.

∼

"DO YOU NEED ANYTHING ELSE?" The hotel clerk says, batting her long eyelashes at Trevor. I don't even mind that she's ignoring that I exist because I know that Trevor is mine.

"No, just a full breakfast in the morning. We've got all we need in each other," he says smiling, his eyes never leaving mine. "We're never going to be apart, ever again."

I giggle as we go up in the elevator at the biggest hotel in the city. This feels like we're teenagers sneaking off to do what we can't do at our parents' homes.

"I think she wanted an autograph," I tease, pushing my hand inside Trevor's coat, feeling his warm body under my fingertips. He flexes his muscles and I gasp at how strong his body is.

"She could have had an autograph if she asked. But that's all that she, or any other woman, can ever have. No one will ever be able to take me away from you."

We rush through the hallway, then fumble with the keycard for the door. When it finally clicks, we're through the door in a flash, pushing it closed behind us.

"Finally. Alone." We both shrug off our coats and let them fall straight to the floor. We rush toward the bed, shedding our clothes as we go.

As I stand, nearly naked in front of Trevor, I feel comfortable in my skin for the first time.

"You are so stunning," he says, his mouth opens as his eyes roam over my body. He caresses my skin and it sends shock-waves through my body. His touch is so reverential and it's so different than how I've felt with other guys. Trevor makes me feel beautiful and desirable.

"You're pretty nice yourself." I smile at him, biting my lip as I look at his muscular body. Years of football has left him more ripped than I thought someone could actually be. I see the scar by his knee and I feel a pang at the loss he's had, but I also feel joy that he's back here now and with me.

"Only pretty nice?" His voice is mock-hurt and it makes me giggle.

"Okay, maybe *very* nice."

"Hmpf."

"Though perhaps I could upgrade my assessment after a bit more…investigation." I let my fingers dance over his skin and reach down to feel his shaft. He's hard and long, and his cock feels glorious.

"Investigation," he says, his voice deepening. "I support investigation."

I shudder as his fingers find my wetness and teases at my clit, massaging it so lightly that flames of desire burn through my body. He wraps his other arm around my waist, holding me close as we stroke and tease each other.

"I want to taste you," he says, and my core flutters at the idea of him between my legs. I bite my lip and nod my head at him, and he walks us over to the bed and gently pushes me down on it. He grabs a pillow and holds it next to my hips. "Put this under your hips."

I lift my hips and he slides the pillow underneath me, and I tremble from how exposed I am to him right now. Trevor stares at my core, a big smile on his lips and his eyes bright with excitement – he looks like a kid ready to devour a birthday cake.

Trevor kneels in front of me, my body shivering as each caress from his tongue moves up my legs and closer to my hot center. When his tongue slides into my wetness, I moan from how exquisite it feels. His tongue circles around my clit, driving me crazy and aching for more.

I've never felt anything so good as this and my body quickly starts tensing and trembling, as I feel an orgasm rapidly building inside my body. I've wanted Trevor for so long and this all feels like the most delicious dream. My senses are on overdrive, as my emotions push me rapidly to a point of explosion.

"Oh!" I cry out as an orgasm suddenly surges through my body, filling me with pleasure as I look down at Trevor. He stares up into my eyes, holding me tightly and slowing his licking, drawing my orgasm out so that I enjoy it longer.

"You taste so good," he says, reaching up to play with one of my breasts as he moves so that his fit body is balanced over mine.

"That was amazing. Your body is so gorgeous," I say, my hands squeezing at the muscles in his arms.

Trevor grins and flexes his muscles over me, and it just makes something in me go weak. This man has the body of a museum statue…and he likes me. No, he *loves* me. I lift my head up to Trevor and kiss him deeply. Tasting myself on his tongue makes me squirm with lust.

"Your body is gorgeous, Mandy. You're the most beautiful woman I've ever seen."

I close my eyes in pleasure as his cock pushes into me and I instantly know that we are a perfect match. His lips claim my mouth in another kiss and our bodies begin rocking together, our rhythm moving faster and faster.

"Damn, you feel so good!" When I look up at Trevor, his eyes are filled with awe as he looks at me. He thrusts deeper and faster into me, and I feel another orgasm building up inside of me.

As Trevor moves faster and faster, I spread my legs farther and push my hips up to him, inviting him to plunge deeper inside of me. His big cock fills me perfectly and I wiggle my hips in joy as he thrusts against my g-spot over and over.

"I'm not going to last much longer," I moan, wrapping my arms around him and holding him tightly.

"Me, neither." Trevor begins thrusting faster and it takes my breath away. Each thrust hits all of my nerve endings in just the right way and then my orgasm is so close and I hear myself crying out and bucking my body against his, desperately aching for release.

"Oh, Trevor! I love you so much!" I moan his name over and over as my second orgasm crashes over me.

"I love...you!" Trevor thrusts deep inside of me and stays there as his body shakes and he groans in pleasure.

My body shaking, I hold Trevor tightly to me. He collapses at my side and then immediately wraps his arms around me and holds me in a fierce bearhug. I snuggle into his embrace, my head against his chest, his rapidly beating heart slowing down as he catches his breath. For the first time in I don't know how long, I feel loved and like I know where I fit in the world. I fit with Trevor.

"I think I'm going to like moving back home." I smile as I look up into Trevor's eyes. This moment feels more perfect than any moment I've ever experienced. I feel wanted and loved. Being with Trevor feels like home.

"If there's anything I can do to help you stay even longer..." There's a wicked smile on Trevor's lips and it sends me into a fit of giggles.

"Your love is enough to make me follow you anywhere, Trevor. I know, now, why it never worked out with anybody else. It's because they weren't you."

The look on Trevor's face softens and his lips find mine and he kisses me slowly. It feels magical to know that I've finally found my one true love.

"It's the same for me, too. I always knew it was you, but I was so scared of your brother."

I roll over so that I'm straddling Trevor's muscular body and I wiggle my hips.

"And I think we need to make up for lost time. Don't you?"

"Absolutely! I'm never letting you get away, ever again."

Thank you so much for reading Unwrapping Her Curves!
If you enjoyed this book, please consider leaving a review or rating on your favorite retailer, Bookbub, or Goodreads!
Thank you!!

**Want an exclusive bonus scene with Trevor and Mandy?
Sign up for my mailing list!**
http://eepurl.com/dh59Xr
**Subscribers receive updates on new books and sales, plus
exclusive bonus content!**

FOR A FULL LISTING of my books, please visit:

https://www.loveheartbooks.com

www.ingramcontent.com/pod-product-compliance
Lightning Source LLC
Chambersburg PA
CBHW071245130726
47998CB00003B/1067